Jamal and the Large Mirror

Written by: **Yancy Seals** • Illustrated by: **Brian Rivera**

To order additional copies of this book, contact:
Xlibris
844-714-8691
www.Xlibris.com
Orders@Xlibris.com

ISBN: Softcover   978-1-6698-4762-5
         Hardcover   978-1-6698-4763-2
         EBook   978-1-6698-4761-8

Print information available on the last page

Rev. date: 09/20/2022

Jamal lived in one of the large Brownstones at 1072 Putnam Ave in Brooklyn NY. He was a very smart little boy with many friends; he was in the fifth grade at Garrett Morgan elementary school, where he loved to play soccer.

1

He lived with his mom and big brother. Jamal's mom was the manager at the neighborhood store, also called the Bodega. Malcolm, Jamal's big brother was fourteen years old, and a freshman at George Washington Carver high school just a few blocks from Jamal's school.

When Jamal was only nine years old his father was killed in a helicopter accivdent in the Iraq war, while serving his country Honorably and proudly, he was also awarded the Purple Heart.

Jamal was so amazed by the awesomeness of the huge mirror, which his father told him was a family heirloom that has been passed down from generation to generation.

4

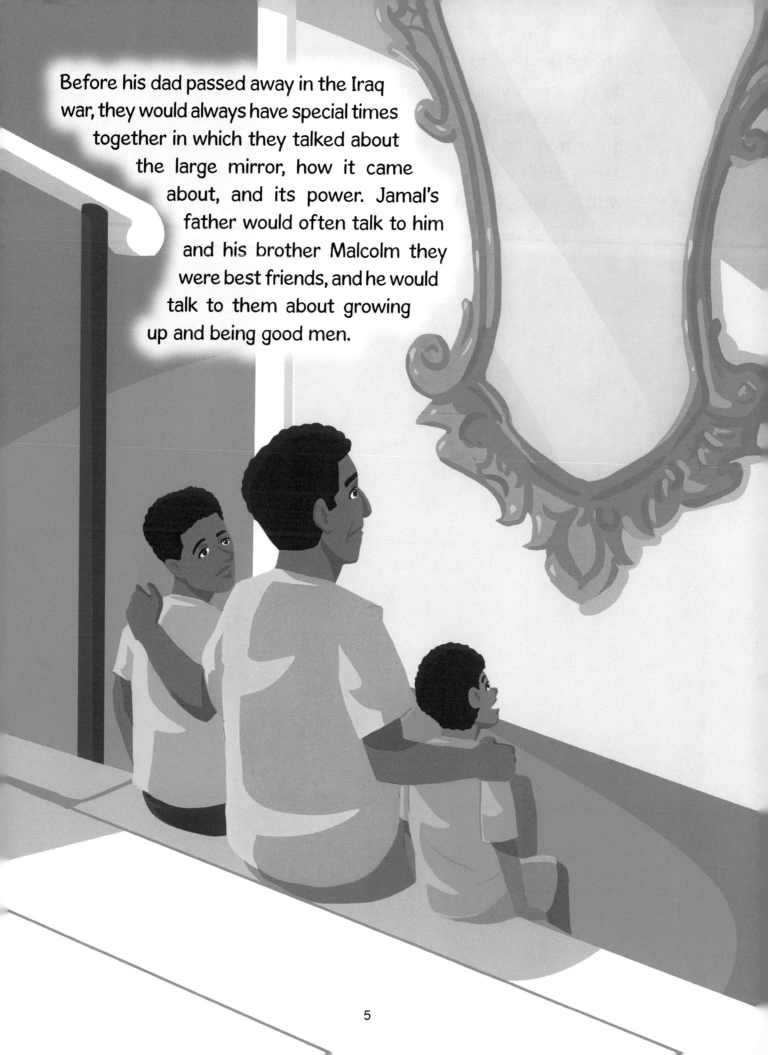

Before his dad passed away in the Iraq war, they would always have special times together in which they talked about the large mirror, how it came about, and its power. Jamal's father would often talk to him and his brother Malcolm they were best friends, and he would talk to them about growing up and being good men.

Things like how to live life without expectations from others, no one owes you anything. If you want it, earn it. Things just don't happen to you, they happen for you, so you can learn and grow from them, and too much is given, much is expected. Jamal didn't understand everything, but the thing that stuck with him was, that it is important to always do your very best, and there's nothing you can't do.

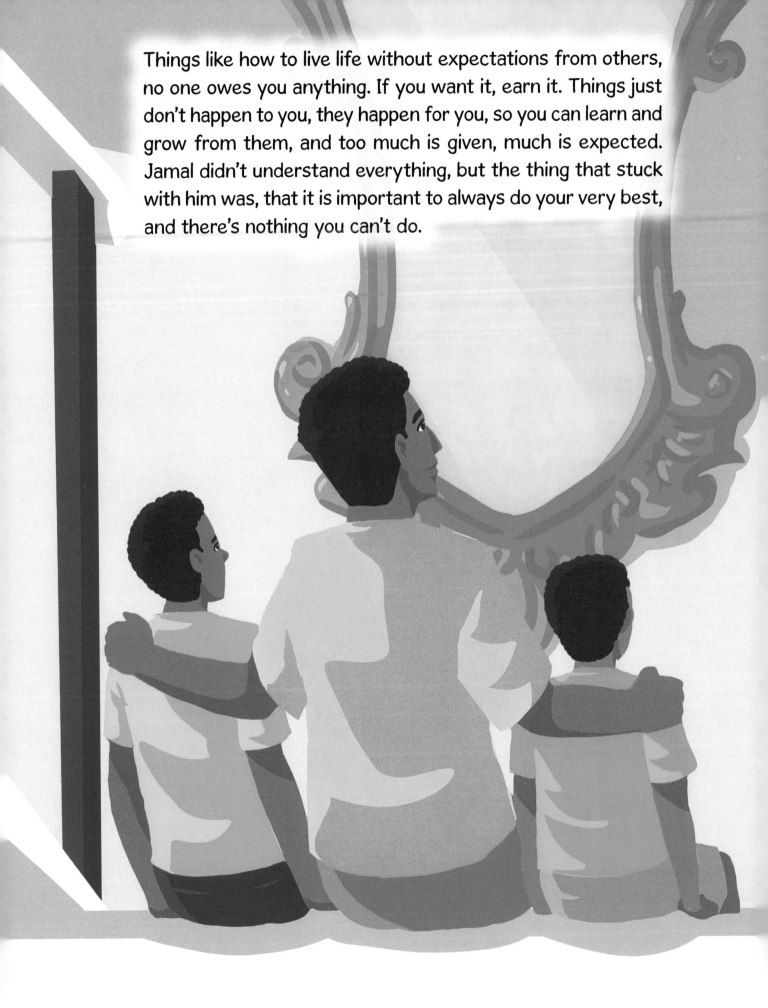

One day Jamal's father was on his way to work at the Military Base, he was to receive orders to go to Iraq, and would be leaving the following week. When coming downstairs and saw Jamal standing in front of the huge mirror fixing his clothing. He decided to use this moment as a teaching moment.

Jamal, his father asked, do you know what this mirror symbolizes and why we draw strength from it? Jamal answered no. Well, he said, the mirror is not just for making sure you look ok. It reminds and helps you to remember the community of people that surrounds you.

Before I walk out the door, I look into the mirror straighten myself and speak. "If it is to be is up to me and it starts with me" the guy in the mirror. And his dad went on to say that there is a large community of people standing behind us so we don't have to be scared, even if I'm no longer here, you can always draw strength from those behind you in the mirror.

Three weeks have passed and while walking home from school with Malcomb, something Jamal enjoyed spending time with his brother. They were only a few houses from home when they saw the Military Soldiers at their door speaking to their mom. Jamal could see one of them handing their mom a flag

Bodega Supermarket

When they arrived home their mom was very upset and crying, however, she managed to tell them the sad news, that their dad was killed in a helicopter accident. Everyone was extremely sad!

Over the last few days, several people have come by the house offering condolences and bringing food. Many military people and a few people from the grocery store where Jamal's mom worked, everyone offering help and telling heartwarming stories, saying how much of a hero my dad was. The community came together during this tough time.

After everyone has gone home, and the music and lights are turned off, the home tends to get very quiet. This is when you start to miss your dad, and you start to wonder exactly how you are going to move on without your best friend.

Jamal tried to remember some of the encouraging things that his dad told him while growing up, like; if it's to be it's up to me, and be your best person, but the pain of missing my dad was still there.

One day Jamal came downstairs and saw his mother, just sitting, deep in thought. Jamal jumped on the couch beside her, what are you thinking about? She said thinking about your dad, his smile, the time we had together, and the family we made. Jamal said I miss him also. Does time heal all hurt, ask Jamal.

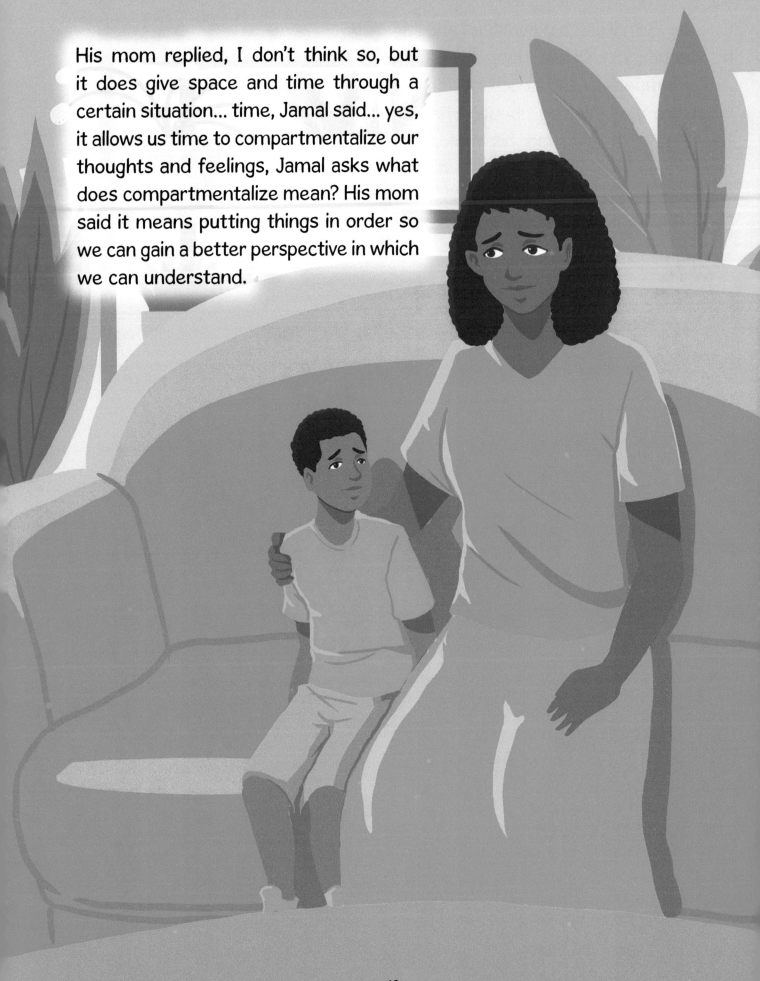

His mom replied, I don't think so, but it does give space and time through a certain situation... time, Jamal said... yes, it allows us time to compartmentalize our thoughts and feelings, Jamal asks what does compartmentalize mean? His mom said it means putting things in order so we can gain a better perspective in which we can understand.

Over the next few days as Jamal came downstairs and he stopped in front of the large mirror to adjust himself to ensure that he was looking well, and his clothes were on straight. Jamal started to remember some of the things that his father always told him, as he looked into the mirror,

So, he stood up straight looked
directly into the mirror, and recited
if it's to be it's up to me, and "I can do
all things through Him that strengthens
me, and no one owes me anything, if
I want it, I must earn it.

And with those last words, Jamal could almost envision in the mirror the community of people that are upholding and standing behind him, he saw his father, Barack Obama, Kamala Harris, Ketanji Brown Jackson, Martin Luther King Jr, and the rest of the community.

This gave Jamal so much strength and belief that he can walk tall and hold his head up because he is the son of an American Hero.

CPSIA information can be obtained
at www.ICGtesting.com
Printed in the USA
BVHW022155260922
648067BV00002B/10